Through the Dragon Glass

and other short stories

by

Abraham Merritt

Contents

Through the Dragon Glass

Herndon helped loot the Forbidden City when the Allies turned the suppression of the Boxers into the most gorgeous burglar-party since the days of Tamerlane. Six of his sailormen followed faithfully his buccaneering fancy. A sympathetic Russian highness whom he had entertained in New York saw to it that he got to the coast and his yacht. That is why Herndon was able to sail through the Narrows with as much of the Son of Heaven's treasures as the most accomplished laborer in Peking's mission vineyards.

Some of the loot he gave to charming ladies who had dwelt or were still dwelling on the sunny side of his heart. Most of it he used to fit up those two astonishing Chinese rooms in his Fifth Avenue house. And a little of it, following a vague religious impulse, he presented to the Metropolitan Museum. This, somehow, seemed to put the stamp of legitimacy on his part of the pillage, like offerings to the gods and building hospitals and peace palaces and such things.

But the Dragon Glass, because he had never seen anything quite so wonderful, he set up in his bedroom Where he could look at it the first thing in the morning, and he placed shaded lights about it so that he could wake up in the night and look at it! Wonderful? It is more than wonderful, the Dragon Glass! Whoever made it lived when the gods walked about the earth creating something new every day. Only a man who lived in that sort of atmosphere could have wrought it. There was never anything like it.

I was in Hawaii when the cables told of Herndon's first disappearance. There wasn't much to tell. His man had gone to his room to awaken him one morning, and Herndon wasn't there. All his clothes were, though. Everything was just as if Herndon ought to be somewhere in the house - only he wasn't.

A man worth ten millions can't step out into thin air and vanish without leaving behind him the probability of some commotion, naturally. The newspapers attend to the commotion, but the columns of type boiled down to essentials contained just two facts: that Herndon had come home the night before, and in the morning he was undiscoverable.

I was on the high seas, homeward bound to help the search, when the wireless told the story of his reappearance. They had found him on the floor of his bedroom, shreds of a silken robe on him, and his body mauled as though by a tiger. But there was no more explanation of his return than there had been of his disappearance.

The night before he hadn't been there and in the morning there he was. Herndon, when he was able to talk, utterly refused to confide even in his doctors. I went straight through to New York, and waited until the men of medicine decided that it was better to let him see me than have him worry any longer about not seeing me.

Herndon got up from a big invalid chair when I entered. His eyes were clear and bright, and there was no weakness in the way he greeted me, nor in the grip of his hand. A nurse slipped from the room.

"What was it, Jim?" I cried. "What on earth happened to you?"

"Not so sure it was on earth," he said. He pointed to what looked like a tall easel hooded with a heavy piece of silk covered with embroidered Chinese characters. He hesitated for a moment and then walked over to a closet. He drew out two heavy-bore guns, the very ones, I remembered, that he had used in his last elephant hunt.

"You won't think me crazy if I ask you to keep one of these handy while I talk, will you, Ward?" he asked rather apologetically. "This looks pretty real, doesn't it?"

He opened his dressing gown and showed me his chest swathed in bandages. He gripped my shoulder as I took without question one of the guns. He walked to the easel and drew off the hood.

"There it is," said Herndon.

And then, for the first time, I saw the Dragon Glass!

2

There never has been anything like that thing! Never! At first all you saw was a cool, green, glimmering translucence, like the sea when you are swimming under water on a still summer day and look up through it. Around its edges ran flickers of scarlet and gold, flashes of emerald, shimmers of silver and ivory. At its base a disk of topaz rimmed with red fire shot up dusky little vaporous yellow flames.

Afterward you were aware that the green translucence was an oval slice of polished stone. The flashes and flickers became dragons. There were twelve of them. Their eyes were emeralds, their fangs were ivory, their claws were gold. There were scaled dragons, and each scale was so inlaid that the base, green as the primeval jungle, shaded off into vivid scarlet, and the scarlet into tips of gold. Their wings were of silver and vermilion, and were folded close to their bodies.

But they were alive, those dragons. There was never so much life in metal and wood since Al-Akram, the Sculptor of ancient Ad, carved the first crocodile, and the jealous Almighty breathed life into it for a punishment!

And last you saw that the topaz disk that sent up the little yellow flames was the top of a metal sphere around which coiled a thirteenth dragon, thin and red, and biting its scorpion-tipped tail.

It took your breath away, the first glimpse of the Dragon Glass. Yes, and the second and third glimpse, too and every other time you looked at it.

"Where did you get it?" I asked, a little shakily.

Herndon said evenly: "It was in a small hidden crypt in the Imperial Palace. We broke into the crypt quite by", he hesitated, "well, call it accident. As soon as I saw it I knew I must have it. What do you think of it?"

"Think!" I cried. "Think! Why, it's the most marvelous thing that the hands of man ever made! What is that stone? Jade?"

"I'm not sure," said Herndon. "But come here. Stand just in front of me."

He switched out the lights in the room. He turned another switch, and on the glass opposite me three shaded electrics threw their rays into its mirror-like oval.

"Watch!" said Herndon. "Tell me what you see!"

3

I looked into the glass. At first I could see nothing but the rays shining farther, farther, back into infinite distances, it seemed. And then.

"Good God!" I cried, stiffening with horror. "Jim, what hellish thing is this?"

"Steady, old man," came Herndon's voice. There was relief and a curious sort of joy in it. "Steady; tell me what you see."

I said: "I seem to see through infinite distances and yet what I see is as close to me as though it were just on the other side of the glass. I see a cleft that cuts through two masses of darker green. I see a claw, a gigantic, hideous claw that stretches out through the cleft. The claw has seven talons that open and close - open and close. Good God, such a claw, Jim! It is like the claws that reach out from the holes in the lama's hell to grip the blind souls as they shudder by!"

"Look, look farther, up through the cleft, above the claw. It widens. What do you see?"

I said: "I see a peak rising enormously high and cutting the sky like a pyramid. There are flashes of flame that dart from behind and outline it. I see a great globe of light like a moon that moves slowly out of the flashes; there is another moving across the breast of the peak; there is a third that swims into the flame at the farthest edge."

"The seven moons of Rak," whispered Herndon, as though to himself. "The seven moons that bathe in the rose flames of Rak which are the fires of life and that circle Lalil like a diadem. He upon whom the seven moons of Rak have shone is bound to Lalil for this life, and for ten thousand lives."

He reached over and turned the switch again. The lights of the room sprang up.

"Jim," I said, "it can't be real! What is it? Some devilish illusion in the glass?"

He unfastened the bandages about his chest.

"The claw you saw had seven talons," he answered quietly. "Well, look at this."

Across the white flesh of his breast, from left shoulder to the lower ribs on the right, ran seven healing furrows. They looked as though they had been made by a gigantic steel comb that had been drawn across him. They gave one the thought they had been ploughed.

"The claw made these," he said as quietly as before.

4

"Ward," he went on, before I could speak, "I wanted you to see - what you've seen. I didn't know whether you would see it. I don't know whether you'll believe me even now. I don't suppose I would if I were in your place...still..."

He walked over and threw the hood upon the Dragon Glass.

"I'm going to tell you," he said. "I'd like to go through it... uninterrupted. That's why I cover it.

"I don't suppose," he began slowly."I don't suppose, Ward, that you've ever heard of Rak the Wonder-Worker, who lived somewhere back at the beginning of things, nor how the Greatest Wonder-Worker banished him somewhere outside the world?"

"No," I said shortly, still shaken by the sight.

"It's a big part of what I've got to tell you," he went on. "Of course you'll think it rot, but... I came across the legend in Tibet first. Then I ran across it again - with the names changed, of course - when I was getting away from China.

"I take it that the gods were still fussing around close to man when Rak was born. The story of his parentage is somewhat scandalous. When he grew older Rak wasn't satisfied with just seeing wonderful things being done. He wanted to do them himself, and he... well, he studied the method. After a while the Greatest Wonder-Worker ran across some of the things Rak had made, and he found them admirable... a little too admirable. He didn't like to destroy the lesser wonder-worker because, so the gossip ran, he felt a sort of responsibility. So he gave Rak a place somewhere - outside the world - and he gave him power over every one out of so many millions of births to lead or lure or sweep that soul into his domain so that he might build up a people - and over his people Rak was given the high, the low, and the middle justice.

"And outside the world Rak went. He fenced his domain about with clouds. He raised a great mountain, and on its flank he built a city for the men and women who were to be his. He circled the city with wonderful gardens, and he placed in the gardens many things, some good and some very terrible. He set around the mountain's brow seven moons for a diadem, and he fanned behind the mountain a fire which is the fire of life, and through which the moons pass eternally to be born again." Herndon's voice sank to a whisper.

5

"Through which the moons pass," he said. "And with them the souls of the people of Rak. They pass through the fires and are born again and again for ten thousand lives. I have seen the moons of Rak and the souls that march with them into the fires. There is no sun in the land, only the new-born moons that shine green on the city and on the gardens."

"Jim," I cried impatiently. "What in the world are you talking about? Wake up, man! What's all that nonsense got to do with this?"

I pointed to the hooded Dragon Glass.

"That," he said. "Why, through that lies the road to the gardens of Rak!"

The heavy gun dropped from my hand as I stared at him, and from him to the glass and back again. He smiled and pointed to his bandaged breast.

He said: "I went straight through to Peking with the Allies. I had an idea what was coming, and I wanted to be in at the death. I was among the first to enter the Forbidden City. I was as mad for loot as any of them. It was a maddening sight, Ward. Soldiers with their arms full of precious stuff even Morgan couldn't buy; soldiers with wonderful necklaces around their hairy throats and their pockets stuffed with jewels; soldiers with their shirts bulging treasures the Sons of Heaven had been hoarding for centuries! We were Goths sacking imperial Rome. Alexander's hosts pillaging that ancient gemmed courtezan of cities, royal Tyre! Thieves in the great ancient scale, a scale so great that it raised even thievery up to something heroic.

"We reached the throne-room. There was a little passage leading off to the left, and my men and I took it. We came into a small octagonal room. There was nothing in it except a very extraordinary squatting figure of jade. It squatted on the floor, its back turned toward us. One of my men stooped to pick it up. He slipped. The figure flew from his hand and smashed into the wall. A slab swung outward. By a... well, call it a fluke, we had struck the secret of the little octagonal room!

"I shoved a light through the aperture. It showed a crypt shaped like a cylinder. The circle of the floor was about ten feet in diameter. The walls were covered with paintings, Chinese characters, queer-looking animals, and things I can't well describe. Around the room, about seven feet up, ran a picture. It showed a sort of island floating off into space.

The clouds lapped its edges like frozen seas full of rainbows. There was a big pyramid of a mountain rising out of the side of it. Around its peak were seven moons, and over the peak... a face!

"I couldn't place that face and I couldn't take my eyes off it. It wasn't Chinese, and it wasn't of any other race I'd ever seen. It was as old as the world and as young as tomorrow. It was benevolent and malicious, cruel and kindly, merciful and merciless, saturnine as Satan and as joyous as Apollo. The eyes were as yellow as buttercups, or as the sunstone on the crest of the Feathered Serpent they worship down in the Hidden Temple of Tuloon. And they were as wise as Fate.

"'There's something else here, sir,' said Martin... you remember Martin, my first officer. He pointed to a shrouded thing on the side. I entered, and took from the thing a covering that fitted over it like a hood. It was the Dragon Glass!

"The moment I saw it I knew I had to have it - and I knew I would have it. I felt that I did not want to get the thing away any more than the thing itself wanted to get away. From the first I thought of the Dragon Glass as something alive. Just as much alive as you and I are. Well, I did get it away. I got it down to the yacht, and then the first odd thing happened.

"You remember Wu-Sing, my boat steward? You know the English Wu-Sing talks. Atrocious! I had the Dragon Glass in my stateroom. I'd forgotten to lock the door. I heard a whistle of sharply indrawn breath. I turned, and there was Wu-Sing. Now, you know that Wu-Sing isn't what you'd call intelligent-looking. Yet as he stood there something seemed to pass over his face, and very subtly change it. The stupidity was wiped out as though a sponge had been passed over it. He did not raise his eyes, but he said, in perfect English, mind you; 'Has the master augustly counted the cost of his possession?'

"I simply gaped at him.

"'Perhaps,' he continued, 'the master has never heard of the illustrious Hao-Tzan? Well, he shall hear.'"

"Ward, I couldn't move or speak. But I know now it wasn't sheer astonishment that held me. I listened while Wu-Sing went on to tell in polished phrase the same story that I had heard in Tibet, only there they called him Rak instead of Hao-Tzan. But it was the same story."

7

"'And,' he finished, 'before he journeyed afar, the illustrious Hao-Tzan caused a great marvel to be wrought. He called it the Gateway.' Wu-Sing waved his hand to the Dragon Glass. 'The master has it. But what shall he who has a Gateway do but pass through it? Is it not better to leave the Gateway behind unless he dare go through it?'"

"He was silent. I was silent, too. All I could do was wonder where the fellow had so suddenly got his command of English. And then Wu-Sing straightened. For a moment his eyes looked into mine. They were as yellow as buttercups, Ward, and wise, wise! My mind rushed back to the little room behind the panel. Ward... The eyes of Wu-Sing were the eyes of the face that brooded over the peak of the moons!"

"And all in a moment, the face of Wu-Sing dropped back into its old familiar stupid lines. The eyes he turned to me were black and clouded. I jumped from my chair."

"'What do you mean, you yellow fraud!' I shouted. 'What do you mean by pretending all this time that you couldn't talk English?'"

"He looked at me stupidly, as usual. He whined in his pidgin that he didn't understand; that he hadn't spoken a word to me until then. I couldn't get anything else out of him, although I nearly frightened his wits out. I had to believe him. Besides, I had seen his eyes. Well, I was fair curious by this time, and I was more anxious to get the glass home safely than ever."

"I got it home. I set it up here, and I fixed those lights as you saw them. I had a sort of feeling that the glass was waiting... for something. I couldn't tell just what. But that it was going to be rather important, I knew."

He suddenly thrust his head into his hands, and rocked to and fro.

"How long, how long," he moaned, "how long, Santhu?"

"Jim!" I cried. "Jim! What's the matter with you?"

He straightened. "In a moment you'll understand," he said.

And then, as quietly as before: "I felt that the glass was waiting. The night I disappeared I couldn't sleep. I turned out the lights in the room; turned them on around the glass and sat before it. I don't know how long I sat, but all at once I jumped to my feet. The dragons seemed to be moving! They were moving! They were crawling round and round the glass. They moved faster and faster. The thirteenth dragon spun

8

about the topaz globe. They circled faster and faster until they were nothing but a halo of crimson and gold flashes. As they spun, the glass itself grew misty, mistier, mistier still, until it was nothing but a green haze. I stepped over to touch it. My hand went straight on through it as though nothing were there.

"I reached in,up to the elbow, up to the shoulder. I felt my hand grasped by warm little fingers. I stepped through... "

"Stepped through the glass?" I cried.

"Through it," he said, "and then... I felt another little hand touch my face. I saw Santhu!

"Her eyes were as blue as the corn flowers, as blue as the big sapphire that shines in the forehead of Vishnu, in his temple at Benares. And they were set wide, wide apart. Her hair was blue-black, and fell in two long braids between her little breasts. A golden dragon crowned her, and through its paws slipped the braids. Another golden dragon girded her. She laughed into my eyes, and drew my head down until my lips touched hers. She was lithe and slender and yielding as the reeds that grow before the Shrine of Hathor that stands on the edge of the Pool of Djeeba. Who Santhu is or where she came from... how do I know? But this I know - she is lovelier than any woman who ever lived on earth. And she is a woman!

"Her arms slipped from about my neck and she drew me forward. I looked about me. We stood in a cleft between two great rocks. The rocks were a soft green, like the green of the Dragon Glass. Behind us was a green mistiness. Before us the cleft ran only a little distance. Through it I saw an enormous peak jutting up like a pyramid, high, high into a sky of chrysoprase. A soft rose radiance pulsed at its sides, and swimming slowly over its breast was a huge globe of green fire. The girl pulled me towards the opening. We walked on silently, hand in hand. Quickly it came to me. Ward, I was in the place whose pictures had been painted in the room of the Dragon Glass!

"We came out of the cleft and into a garden. The Gardens of Many-Columned Iram, lost in the desert because they were too beautiful, must have been like that place. There were strange, immense trees whose branches were like feathery plumes and whose plumes shone with fires like those that clothe the feet of Indra's dancers. Strange flowers raised themselves along our path, and their hearts glowed like the glow-worms

9

that are fastened to the rainbow bridge to Asgard. A wind sighed through the plumed trees, and luminous shadows drifted past their trunks. I heard a girl laugh, and the voice of a man singing.

"We went on. Once there was a low wailing far in the garden, and the girl threw herself before me, her arms outstretched. The wailing ceased, and we went on. The mountain grew plainer. I saw another great globe of green fire swing out of the rose flashes at the right of the peak. I saw another shining into the glow at the left. There was a curious trail of mist behind it. It was a mist that had tangled in it a multitude of little stars. Everything was bathed in a soft green light, such a light as you would have if you lived within a pale emerald.

"We turned and went along another little trail. The little trail ran up a little hill, and on the hill was a little house. It looked as though it was made of ivory. It was a very odd little house. It was more like the Jain pagodas at Brahmaputra than anything else. The walls glowed as though they were full light. The girl touched the wall, and a panel slid away. We entered, and the panel closed after us.

"The room was filled with a whispering yellow light. I say whispering because that is how one felt about it. It was gentle and alive. A stairway of ivory ran up to another room above. The girl pressed me toward it. Neither of us had uttered a word. There was a spell of silence upon me. I could not speak. There seemed to be nothing to say. I felt a great rest and a great peace, as though I had come home. I walked up the stairway and into the room above. It was dark except for a bar of green light that came through the long and narrow window. Through it I saw the mountain and its moons. On the floor was an ivory head-rest and some silken cloths. I felt suddenly very sleepy. I dropped to the cloths, and at once was asleep.

"When I awoke the girl with the cornflower eyes was beside me! She was sleeping. As I watched, her eyes opened. She smiled and drew me to her."

"I do not know why, but a name came to me. 'Santhu!' I cried. She smiled again, and I knew that I had called her name. It seemed to me that I remembered her, too, out of immeasurable ages. I arose and walked to the window. I looked toward the mountain. There were now two moons on its breast. And then I saw the city that lay on the mountain's flank. It was such a city as you see in dreams, or as the tale-tellers

10

of El-Bahara fashion out of the mirage. It was all of ivory and shining greens and flashing blues and crimsons. I could see people walking about its streets. There came the sound of little golden bells chiming.

"I turned toward the girl. She was sitting up, her hands clasped about her knees, watching me. Love came, swift and compelling. She arose.I took her in my arms.

"Many times the moons circled the mountains, and the mist held the little, tangled stars passing with them. I saw no one but Santhu; no thing came near us. The trees fed us with fruits that had in them the very essences of life. Yes, the fruit of the Tree of Life that stood in Eden must have been like the fruit of those trees. We drank of green water that sparkled with green fires, and tasted like the wine Osiris gives the hungry souls in Amenti to strengthen them. We bathed in pools of carved stone that welled with water yellow as amber. Mostly we wandered in the gardens. There were many wonderful things in the gardens. They were very unearthly. There was no day nor night. Only the green glow of the ever-circling moons. We never talked to each other. I don't know why. Always there seemed nothing to say.

"Then Santhu began to sing to me. Her songs were strange songs. I could not tell what the words were. But they built up pictures in my brain. I saw Rak the Wonder-Worker fashioning his gardens, and filling them with things beautiful and things... evil. I saw him raise the peak, and knew that it was Lalil; saw him fashion the seven moons and kindle the fires that are the fires of life. I saw him build his city, and I saw men and women pass into it from the world through many gateways.

"Santhu sang and I knew that the marching stars in the mist were the souls of the people of Rak which sought rebirth. She sang, and I saw myself ages past walking in the city of Rak with Santhu beside me. Her song wailed, and I felt myself one of the mist-entangled stars. Her song wept, and I felt myself a star that fought against the mist, and, fighting, break away - a star that fled out and out through immeasurable green space.

"A man stood before us. He was very tall. His face was both cruel and kind, saturnine as Satan and joyous as Apollo. He raised his eyes to us, and they were yellow as buttercups, and wise, so wise! Ward, it was the face above the peak in the room of the Dragon Glass! The eyes that had looked at me out of Wu-Sing's face! He smiled on us for a moment and then... he was gone!

"I took Santhu by the hand and began to run. Quite suddenly it came to me that I had enough of the haunted gardens of Rak; that I wanted to get back to my own land. But not without Santhu. I tried to remember the road to the cleft. I felt that there lay the path back. We ran. From far behind came a wailing. Santhu screamed... but I knew the fear in her cry was not for herself. It was for me. None of the creatures of that place could harm her who was herself one of its creatures. The wailing drew closer. I turned.

"Winging down through the green air was a beast, an unthinkable beast, Ward! It was like the winged beast of the Apocalypse that is to bear the woman arrayed in purple and scarlet. It was beautiful even in its horror. It closed its scarlet and golden wings, and its long, gleaming body shot at me like a monstrous spear.

"And then, just as it was about to strike - a mist threw itself between us! It was a rainbow mist, and it was cast. It was cast as though a hand had held it and thrown it like a net. I heard the winged beast shriek its disappointment, Santhu's hand gripped mine tighter. We ran through the mist.

"Before us was the cleft between the two green rocks. Time and time again we raced for it, and time and time again that beautiful shining horror struck at me and each time came the thrown mist to baffle it. It was a game! Once I heard a laugh, and then I knew who was my hunter. The master of the beast and the caster of the mist. It was he of the yellow eyes, and he was playing me, playing me as a child plays with a cat when he tempts it with a piece of meat and snatches the meat away again and again from the hungry jaws!

"The mist cleared away from its last throw, and the mouth of the cleft was just before us. Once more the thing swooped and this time there was no mist. The player had tired of the game! As it struck, Santhu raised herself before it. The beast swerved and the claw that had been stretched to rip me from throat to waist struck me a glancing blow. I fell, fell through leagues and leagues of green space.

"When I awoke I was here in this bed, with the doctor men around me and this." He pointed to his bandaged breast again.

"That night when the nurse was asleep I got up and looked into the Dragon Glass, and I saw the claw, even as you did. The beast is there. It is waiting for me!"

Herndon was silent for a moment.

"If he tires of the waiting he may send the beast through for me," he said. "I mean the man with the yellow eyes. I've a desire to try one of these guns on it. It's real, you know, the beast is… and these guns have stopped elephants."

"But the man with the yellow eyes, Jim," I whispered, "who is he?"

"He," said Herndon, "why, he's the Wonder-Worker himself!"

"You don't believe such a story as that!" I cried. "Why, it's… it's lunacy! It's some devilish illusion in the glass. It's like the crystal globe that makes you hypnotize yourself and think the things your own mind creates are real. Break it, Jim! It's devilish! Break it!"

"Break it!" he said incredulously. "Break it? Not for the ten thousand lives that are the toll of Rak! Not real? Aren't these wounds real? Wasn't Santhu real? Break it! Good God, man, you don't know what you say! Why, it's my only road back to her! If that yellow-eyed devil back there were only as wise as he looks, he would know he didn't have to keep his beast watching there. I want to go, Ward; I want to go and bring her back with me. I've an idea, somehow, that he hasn't…well, full control of things. I've an idea that the Greatest Wonder-Worker wouldn't put wholly in Rak's hands the souls that wander through the many gateways into his kingdom. There's a way out, Ward; there's a way to escape him. I won away from him once, Ward. I'm sure of it. But then I left Santhu behind. I have to go back for her. That's why I found the little passage that led from the throne-room. And he knows it, too. That's why he had to turn his beast on me."

"And I'll go through again, Ward. And I'll come back again… with Santhu!"

But he has not returned. It is six months now since he disappeared for the second time. And from his bedroom, as he had done before. By the will that they found - the will that commended that in event of his disappearing as he had done before and not returning within a week I was to have his house and all that was within it… I came into possession of the Dragon Glass. The dragons had spun again for Hern-

13

don, and he had gone through the gateway once more. I found only one of the elephant guns, and I knew that he had had time to take the other with him.

I sit night after night before the glass, waiting for him to come back through it with Santhu. Sooner or later they will come. That I know.

THE END

The People of the Pit

North of us a shaft of light shot half way to the zenith. It came from behind the five peaks. The beam drove up through a column of blue haze whose edges were marked as sharply as the rain that streams from the edges of a thunder cloud. It was like the flash of a searchlight through an azure mist. It cast no shadows.

As it struck upward the summits were outlined hard and black and I saw that the whole mountain was shaped like a hand. As the light silhouetted it, the gigantic fingers stretched, the hand seemed to thrust itself forward. It was exactly as though it moved to push something back. The shining beam held steady for a moment; then broke into myriads of little luminous globes that swung to and fro and dropped gently. They seemed to be searching.

The forest had become very still. Every wood noise held its breath. I felt the dogs pressing against my legs. They too were silent; but every muscle in their bodies trembled, their hair was stiff along their backs and their eyes, fixed on the falling lights, were filmed with the terror glaze.

I looked at Anderson. He was staring at the North where once more the beam had pulsed upward.

"It can't be the aurora," I spoke without moving my lips. My mouth was as dry as though Lao T'zai had poured his fear dust down my throat.

"If it is I never saw one like it," he answered in the same tone. "Besides who ever heard of an aurora at this time of the year?"

He voiced the thought that was in my own mind.

"It makes me think something is being hunted up there," he said, "an unholy sort of hunt; it's well for us to be out of range."

"The mountain seems to move each time the shaft shoots up," I said. "What's it keeping back, Starr? It makes me think of the frozen hand of cloud that Shan Nadour set before the Gate of Ghouls to keep them in the lairs that Eblis cut for them."

He raised a hand listening.

From the North and high overhead there came a whispering. It was not the rustling of the aurora, that rushing, crackling sound like the ghosts of winds that blew at Creation racing through the skeleton leaves of ancient trees that sheltered Lilith. It was a whispering that held in it a demand. It was eager. It called us to come up where the beam was flashing. It drew. There was in it a note of inexorable insistence. It touched my heart with a thousand tiny fear-tipped fingers and it filled me with a vast longing to race on and merge myself in the light. It must have been so that Ulysses felt when he strained at the mast and strove to obey the crystal sweet singing of the Sirens.

The whispering grew louder.

"What the hell's the matter with those dogs?" cried Anderson savagely. "Look at them!"

The malemutes, whining, were racing away toward the light. We saw them disappear among the trees. There came back to us a mournful howling. Then that too died away and left nothing but the insistent murmuring overhead.

The glade we had camped in looked straight to the North. We had reached I suppose three hundred mile above the first great bend of the Koskokwim toward the Yukon. Certainly we were in an untrodden part of the wilderness. We had pushed through from Dawson at the breaking of the Spring, on a fair lead to the lost five peaks between which, so the Athabasean medicine man had told us, the gold streams out like putty from a clenched fist. Not an Indian were we able to get to go with us. The land of the Hand Mountain was accursed they said. We had sighted the peaks the night before, their tops faintly outlined against a pulsing glow. And now we saw the light that had led us to them.

Anderson stiffened. Through the whispering had broken a curious pad-pad and a rustling. It sounded as though a small bear were

16

moving towards us. I threw a pile of wood on the fire and, as it blazed up, saw something break through the bushes. It walked on all fours, but it did not walk like a bear. All at once it flashed upon me; it was like a baby crawling upstairs. The forepaws lifted themselves in grotesquely infantile fashion. It was grotesque but it was terrible. It grew closer. We reached for our guns and dropped them. Suddenly we knew that this crawling thing was a man!

It was a man. Still with the high climbing pad-pad he swayed to the fire. He stopped.

"Safe," whispered the crawling man, in a voice that was an echo of the murmur overhead. "Quite safe here. They can't get out of the blue, you know. They can't get you unless you go to them."

He fell over on his side. We ran to him. Anderson knelt.

"God's love!" he said. "Frank, look at this!" He pointed to the hands. The wrists were covered with torn rags of a heavy shirt. The hands themselves were stumps! The fingers had been bent into the palms and the flesh had been worn to the bone. They looked like the feet of a little black elephant! My eyes traveled down the body. Around the waist was a heavy band of yellow metal. From it fell a ring and a dozen links of shining white chain!

"What is he? Where did he come from?" said Anderson. "Look, he's fast asleep, yet even in his sleep his arms try to climb and his feet draw themselves up one after the other! And his knees... how in God's name was he ever able to move on them?"

It was even as he said. In the deep sleep that had come upon the crawler arms and legs kept raising in a deliberate, dreadful climbing motion. It was as though they had a life of their own; they kept their movement independently of the motionless body. They were semaphoric motions. If you have ever stood at the back of a train and had watched the semaphores rise and fall you will know exactly what I mean.

Abruptly the overhead whispering ceased. The shaft of light dropped and did not rise again. The crawling man became still. A gentle glow began to grow around us. It was dawn, and the short Alaskan summer night was over. Anderson rubbed his eyes and turned to me a haggard face.

"Man!" he exclaimed. "You look as though you have been through a spell of sickness!"

"No more than you, Starr," I said. "What do you make of it all?"

"I'm thinking our only answer lies there," he answered, pointing to the figure that lay so motionless under the blankets we had thrown over him. "Whatever it was, that's what it was after. There was no aurora about that light, Frank. It was like the flaring up of some queer hell the preacher folk never frightened us with."

"We'll go no further today," I said. "I wouldn't wake him for all the gold that runs between the fingers of the five peaks, nor for all the devils that may be behind them."

The crawling man lay in a sleep as deep as the Styx. We bathed and bandaged the pads that had been his hands. Arms and legs were as rigid as though they were crutches. He did not move while we worked over him. He lay as he had fallen, the arms a trifle raised, the knees bent.

"Why did he crawl?" whispered Anderson. "Why didn't he walk?"

I was filing the band about the waist. It was gold, but it was like no gold I had ever handled. Pure gold is soft. This was soft, but it had an unclean, viscid life of its own. It clung to the file. I gashed through it, bent it away from the body and hurled it far off. It was loathsome!

All that day he slept. Darkness came and still he slept. That night there was no shaft of light, no questing globe, no whispering. Some spell of horror seemed lifted from the land. It was noon when the crawling man awoke. I jumped as the pleasant drawling voice sounded.

"How long have I slept?" he asked. His pale blue eyes grew quizzical as I stared at him. "A night and almost two days," I said. "Was there any light up there last night?" He nodded to the North eagerly. "Any whispering?"

"Neither," I answered. His head fell back and he stared up at the sky.

"They've given it up, then?" he said at last.

"Who have given it up?" asked Anderson.

"Why, the people of the pit," replied the crawling man quietly.

We stared at him. "The people of the pit," he said. "Things that the Devil made before the Flood and that somehow have escaped God's vengeance. You weren't in any danger from them unless you had followed their call. They can't get any further than the blue haze. I was their prisoner," he added simply. "They were trying to whisper me back to them!"

Anderson and I looked at each other, the same thought in both our minds.

"You're wrong," said the crawling man. "I'm not insane. Give me a very little to drink. I'm going to die soon, but I want you to take me as far South as you can before I die, and afterwards I want you to build a big fire and burn me. I want to be in such shape that no infernal spell of theirs can drag my body back to them. You'll do it too, when I've told you about them, " he hesitated. "I think their chain is off me?" he said.

"I cut it off," I answered shortly.

"Thank God for that too," whispered the crawling man.

He drank the brandy and water we lifted to his lips.

"Arms and legs quite dead," he said. "Dead as I'll be soon. Well, they did well for me. Now I'll tell you what's up there behind that hand. Hell!"

"Now listen. My name is Stanton - Sinclair Stanton. Class 1900, Yale. Explorer. I started away from Dawson last year to hunt for five peaks that rise like a hand in a haunted country and run pure gold between them. Same thing you were after? I thought so. Late last fall my comrade sickened. Sent him back with some Indians. Little later all my Indians ran away from me. I decided I'd stick, built a cabin, stocked myself with food and lay down to winter it. In the Spring I started off again. Little less than two weeks ago I sighted the five peaks. Not from this side though, the other. Give me some more brandy.

"I'd made too wide a detour," he went on. "I'd gotten too far North. I beat back. From this side you see nothing but forest straight up to the base of the Hand Mountain. Over on the other side."

He was silent for a moment.

"Over there is forest too. But it doesn't reach so far. No! I came out of it. Stretching miles in front of me was a level plain. It was as worn and ancient looking as the desert around the ruins of Babylon. At its end rose the peaks. Between me and them - far off - was what looked like a low dike of rocks. Then I ran across the road!"

"The road!" cried Anderson incredulously.

"The road," said the crawling man. "A fine smooth stone road. It ran straight on to the mountain. Oh, it was road all right and worn as though millions and millions of feet had passed over it for thousands of years. On each side of it were sand and heaps of stones. After while I began to notice these stones. They were cut, and the shape of the heaps somehow gave me the idea that a hundred thousand years ago they might have been houses. I sensed man about them and at the same time they smelled of immemorial antiquity. Well...

"The peaks grew closer. The heaps of ruins thicker. Something inexpressibly desolate hovered over them; something reached from them that struck my heart like the touch of ghosts so old that they could be only the ghosts of ghosts. I went on.

"And now I saw that what I had thought to be the low rock range at the base of the peaks was a thicker litter of ruins. The Hand Mountain was really much farther off. The road passed between two high rocks that raised themselves like a gateway."

The crawling man paused.

"They were a gateway," he said. "I reached them. I went between them. And then I sprawled and clutched the earth in sheer awe! I was on a broad stone platform. Before me was...sheer space! Imagine the Grand Canyon five times as wide and with the bottom dropped out. That is what I was looking into. It was like peeping over the edge of a cleft world down into the infinity where the planets roll! On the far side stood the five peaks. They looked like a gigantic warning hand stretched up to the sky. The lip of the abyss curved away on each side of me.

"I could see down perhaps a thousand feet. Then a thick blue haze shut out the eye. It was like the blue you see gather on the high hills at dusk. And the pit it was awesome; awesome as the Maori Gulf of Ra-nalak, that sinks between the living and the dead and that only the freshly released soul has strength to leap but never strength to cross again.

"I crept back from the verge and stood up, weak. My hand rested against one of the pillars of the gateway. There was carving upon it. It bore in still sharp outlines the heroic figure of a man. His back was turned. His arms were outstretched. There was an odd peaked headdress upon him. I looked at the opposite pillar. It bore a figure exactly similar. The pillars were triangular and the carvings were on the side away from the pit. The figures seemed to be holding something back. I looked closer. Behind the outstretched hands I seemed to see other shapes.

"I traced them out vaguely. Suddenly I felt unaccountably sick. There had come to me an impression of enormous upright slugs. Their swollen bodies were faintly cut, all except the heads which were well marked globes. They were unutterably loathsome. I turned from the gates back to the void. I stretched myself upon the slab and looked over the edge.

"A stairway led down into the pit!"

"A stairway!" we cried.

"A stairway," repeated the crawling man as patiently as before. "It seemed not so much carved out of the rock as built into it. The slabs were about six feet long and three feet wide. It ran down from the platform and vanished into the blue haze."

"But who could build such a stairway as that?" I said. "A stairway built into the wall of a precipice and leading down into a bottomless pit!"

"Not bottomless," said the crawling man quietly. "There was a bottom. I reached it!"

"Reached it?" we repeated.

"Yes, by the stairway," answered the crawling man. "You see... I went down it!

"Yes," he said. "I went down the stairway. But not that day. I made my camp back of the gates. At dawn I filled my knapsack with food, my two canteens with water from a spring that wells up there by the gateway, walked between the carved monoliths and stepped over the edge of the pit.

"The steps ran along the side of the rock at a forty degree pitch. As I went down and down I studied them. They were of a greenish rock quite different from the granitic porphyry that formed the wall of the precipice. At first I thought that the builders had taken advantage of an outcropping stratum, and had carved from it their gigantic flight. But the regularity of the angle at which it fell made me doubtful of this theory.

"After I had gone perhaps half a mile I stepped out upon a landing. From this landing the stairs made a V shaped turn and ran on downward, clinging to the cliff at the same angle as the first flight; it was a zig-zag, and after I had made three of these turns I knew that the steps dropped straight down in a succession of such angles. No strata could be so regular as that. No, the stairway was built by hands! But whose? The answer is in those ruins around the edge, I think... never to be read.

"By noon I had lost sight of the five peaks and the lip of the abyss. Above me, below me, was nothing but the blue haze. Beside me, too, was nothingness, for the further breast of rock had long since vanished. I felt no dizziness, and any trace of fear was swallowed in a vast curiosity. What was I to discover? Some ancient and wonderful civilization that had ruled when the Poles were tropical gardens? Nothing living, I felt sure; all was too old for life. Still, a stairway so wonderful must lead to something quite as wonderful I knew. What was it? I went on.

"At regular intervals I had passed the mouths of small caves. There would be two thousand steps and then an opening, two thousand more steps and an opening, and so on and on. Late that afternoon I stopped before one of these clefts. I suppose I had gone then three miles down the pit, although the angles were such that I had walked in all fully ten miles. I examined the entrance. On each side were carved the figures of the great portal above, only now they were standing face forward, the arms outstretched as though to hold something back from the outer depths. Their faces were covered with veils. There were no hideous shapes behind them. I went inside. The fissure ran back for twenty yards like a burrow. It was dry and perfectly light. Outside I could see the blue haze rising upward like a column, its edges clearly marked. I felt an extraordinary sense of security, although I had not been conscious of any fear. I felt that the figures at the entrance were guardians, but against what?

"The blue haze thickened and grew faintly luminescent. I fancied that it was dusk above. I ate and drank a little and slept. When I awoke the blue had lightened again, and I fancied it was dawn above. I went on. I forgot the gulf yawning at my side. I felt no fatigue and little hunger or thirst, although I had drunk and eaten sparingly. That night I spent within another of the caves, and at dawn I descended again.

"It was late that day when I first saw the city."

He was silent for a time.

"The city," he said at last, "there is a city you know. But not such a city as you have ever seen; nor any other man who has lived to tell of it. The pit, I think, is shaped like a bottle; the opening before the five peaks is the neck. But how wide the bottom is I do not know; thousands of miles maybe. I had begun to catch little glints of light far down in the blue. Then I saw the tops of trees, I suppose they are. But not our kind of trees - unpleasant, snaky kind of trees. They reared themselves on high thin trunks and their tops were nests of thick tendrils with ugly little leaves like arrow heads. The trees were red, a vivid angry red. Here and there I glimpsed spots of shining yellow. I knew these were water because I could see things breaking through their surface; or at least I could see the splash and ripple, but what it was that disturbed them I never saw.

"Straight beneath me was the city. I looked down upon mile after mile of closely packed cylinders. They lay upon their sides in pyramids of three, of five, of dozens, piled upon each other. It is hard to make you see what that city is like; look, suppose you have water pipes of a certain length and first you lay three of them side by side and on top of them you place two and on these two one; or suppose you take five for a foundation and place on these four and then three, then two and then one. Do you see? That was the way they looked. But they were topped by towers, by minarets, by flares, by fans, and twisted monstrosities. They gleamed as though coated with pale rose flame. Beside them the venomous red trees raised themselves like the heads of hydras guarding nests of gigantic, jeweled and sleeping worms!

"A few feet beneath me the stairway jutted out into a Titanic arch, unearthly as the span that bridges Hell and leads to Asgard. It curved out and down straight through the top of the highest pile of carven cylinders and then it vanished through it. It was appalling; it was demonic."

The crawling man stopped. His eyes rolled up into his head. He trembled and his arms and legs began their horrible crawling movement. From his lips came a whispering. It was an echo of the high murmuring we had heard the night he came to us. I put my hands over his eyes. He quieted.

"The Things Accursed!" he said. "The People of the Pit! Did I whisper. Yes, but they can't get me now, they can't!"

After a time he began as quietly as before.

"I crossed the span. I went down through the top of that building. Blue darkness shrouded me for a moment and I felt the steps twist into a spiral. I wound down and then I was standing high up in; I can't

23

tell you in what, I'll have to call it a room. We have no images for what is in the pit. A hundred feet below me was the floor. The walls sloped down and out from where I stood in a series of widening crescents. The place was colossal and it was filled with a curious mottled red light. It was like the light inside a green and gold flecked fire opal. I went down to the last step. Far in front of me rose a high, columned altar. Its pillars were carved in monstrous scrolls, like mad octopuses with a thousand drunken tentacles; they rested on the backs of shapeless monstrosities carved in crimson stone. The altar front was a gigantic slab of purple covered with carvings.

"I can't describe these carvings! No human being could; the human eye cannot grasp them any more than it can grasp the shapes that haunt the fourth dimension. Only a subtle sense in the back of the brain sensed them vaguely. They were formless things that gave no conscious image, yet pressed into the mind like small hot seals - ideas of hate, of combats between unthinkable monstrous things; victories in a nebulous hell of steaming, obscene jungles; aspirations and ideals immeasurably loathsome.

"And as I stood I grew aware of something that lay behind the lip of the altar fifty feet above me. I knew it was there. I felt it with every hair and every tiny bit of my skin. Something infinitely malignant, infinitely horrible, infinitely ancient. It lurked, it brooded, it threatened and it was invisible!

"Behind me was a circle of blue light. I ran for it. Something urged me to turn back, to climb the stairs and make away. It was impossible. Repulsion for that unseen Thing raced me onward as though a current had my feet. I passed through the circle. I was out on a street that stretched on into dim distance between rows of the carven cylinders.

"Here and there the red trees arose. Between them rolled the stone burrows. And now I could take in the amazing ornamentation that clothed them. They were like the trunks of smooth skinned trees that had fallen and had been clothed with high reaching noxious orchids. Yes, those cylinders were like that, and more. They should have gone out with the dinosaurs. They were monstrous. They struck the eyes like a blow and they passed across the nerves like a rasp. And nowhere was there sight or sound of living thing.

"There were circular openings in the cylinders like the circle in the Temple of the Stairway. I passed through one of them. I was in a long, bare vaulted room whose curving sides half closed twenty feet over my head, leaving a wide slit that opened into another vaulted chamber above. There was absolutely nothing in the room save the same mottled reddish light that I had seen in the Temple. I stumbled. I still could see nothing, but there was something on the floor over which I had tripped. I reached down and my hand touched a thing cold and smooth that moved under it. I turned and ran out of that place. I was filled with a loathing that had in it something of madness. I ran on and on blindly wringing my hands weeping with horror.

"When I came to myself I was still among the stone cylinders and red trees. I tried to retrace my steps; to find the Temple. I was more than afraid. I was like a new loosed soul panic-stricken with the first terrors of hell. I could not find the Temple! Then the haze began to thicken and glow; the cylinders to shine more brightly. I knew that it was dusk in the world above and I felt that with dusk my time of peril had come; that the thickening of the haze was the signal for the awakening of whatever things lived in this pit.

"I scrambled up the sides of one of the burrows. I hid behind a twisted nightmare of stone. Perhaps, I thought, there was a chance of remaining hidden until the blue lightened and the peril passed. There began to grow around me a murmur. It was everywhere and it grew and grew into a great whispering. I peeped from the side of the stone down into the street. I saw lights passing and repassing. More and more lights. They swam out of the circular doorways and they thronged the street. The highest were eight feet above the pave; the lowest perhaps two. They hurried, they sauntered, they bowed, they stopped and whispered and there was nothing under them!"

"Nothing under them!" breathed Anderson.

"No," he went on, "that was the terrible part of it; there was nothing under them. Yet certainly the lights were living things. They had consciousness, volition, thought - what else I did not know. They were nearly two feet across, the largest. Their center was a bright nucleus; red, blue, green. This nucleus faded off, gradually, into a misty glow that did not end abruptly. It too seemed to fade off into nothingness, but a nothingness that had under it a somethingness. I strained my eyes trying to

25

grasp this body into which the lights merged and which one could only feel was there, but could not see.

"And all at once I grew rigid. Something cold, and thin like a whip, had touched my face. I turned my head. Close behind were three of the lights. They were a pale blue. They looked at me if you can imagine lights that are eyes. Another whiplash gripped my shoulder. Under the closest light came a shrill whispering. I shrieked. Abruptly the murmuring in the street ceased. I dragged my eyes from the pale blue globe that held them and looked out; the lights in the streets were rising by myriads to the level of where I stood! There they stopped and peered at me. They crowded and jostled as though they were a crowd of curious people on Broadway. I felt a score of the lashes touch me.

"When I came to myself I was again in the great Place of the Stairway, lying at the foot of the altar. All was silent. There were no lights, only the mottled red glow. I jumped to my feet and ran toward the steps. Something jerked me back to my knees. And then I saw that around my waist had been fastened a yellow ring of metal. From it hung a chain and this chain passed up over the lip of the high ledge. I was chained to the altar!

"I reached into my pockets for my knife to cut through the ring. It was not there! I had been stripped of everything except one of the canteens that I had hung around my neck and which I suppose. They had thought was part of me. I tried to break the ring. It seemed alive. It writhed in my hands and it drew itself closer around me! I pulled at the chain. It was immovable. There came to me the consciousness of the unseen Thing above the altar. I groveled at the foot of the slab and wept. Think - alone in that place of strange light with the brooding ancient Horror above me; a monstrous Thing, a Thing unthinkable; an unseen Thing that poured forth horror.

"After awhile I gripped myself. Then I saw beside one of the pillars a yellow bowl filled with a thick white liquid. I drank it. If it killed I did not care. But its taste was pleasant and as I drank my strength came back to me with a rush. Clearly I was not to be starved. The lights, whatever they were, had a conception of human needs.

"And now the reddish mottled gleam began to deepen. Outside arose the humming and through the circle that was the entrance came streaming the globes. They ranged themselves in ranks until they filled the Temple. Their whispering grew into a chant, a cadenced whispering chant that rose and fell, rose and fell, while to its rhythm the globes lifted and sank, lifted and sank.

"All that night the lights came and went and all that night the chant sounded as they rose and fell. At the last I felt myself only an atom of consciousness in a sea of cadenced whispering; an atom that rose and fell with the bowing globes. I tell you that even my heart pulsed in unison with them! The red glow faded, the lights streamed out; the whispering died. I was again alone and I knew that once again day had broken in my own world.

"I slept. When I awoke I found beside the pillar more of the white liquid. I scrutinized the chain that held me to the altar. I began to rub two of the links together. I did this for hours. When the red began to thicken there was a ridge worn in the links. Hope rushed up within me. There was, then, a chance to escape.

"With the thickening the lights came again. All through that night the whispering chant sounded, and the globes rose and fell. The chant seized me. It pulsed through me until every nerve and muscle quivered to it. My lips began to quiver. They strove like a man trying to cry out on a nightmare. And at last they too were whispering the chant of the people of the pit. My body bowed in unison with the lights. I was, in movement and sound, one with the nameless things while my soul sank back sick with horror and powerless. While I whispered I saw Them!"

"Saw the lights?" I asked stupidly.

"Saw the Things under the lights," he answered. "Great transparent snail-like bodies, dozens of waving tentacles stretching from them, round gaping mouths under the luminous seeing globes. They were like the ghosts of inconceivably monstrous slugs! I could see through them. And as I stared, still bowing and whispering, the dawn came and they streamed to and through the entrance. They did not crawl or walk; they floated! They floated and were gone!

"I did not sleep. I worked all that day at my chain. By the thickening of the red I had worn it a sixth through. And all that night I whispered and bowed with the pit people, joining in their chant to the Thing that brooded above me!

"Twice again the red thickened and the chant held me, then on the morning of the fifth day I broke through the worn links of the chain.

27

I was free! I drank from the bowl of white liquid and poured what was left in my flask. I ran to the Stairway. I rushed up and past that unseen Horror behind the altar ledge and was out upon the Bridge. I raced across the span and up the Stairway.

"Can you think what it is to climb straight up the verge of a cleft-world with hell behind you? Hell was behind me and terror rode me. The city had long been lost in the blue haze before I knew that I could climb no more. My heart beat upon my ears like a sledge. I fell before one of the little caves feeling that here at last was sanctuary. I crept far back within it and waited for the haze to thicken. Almost at once it did so. From far below me came a vast and angry murmur. At the mouth of the rift I saw a light pulse up through the blue; die down and as it dimmed I saw myriads of the globes that are the eyes of the pit people swing downward into the abyss. Again and again the light pulsed and the globes fell. They were hunting me. The whispering grew louder, more insistent.

"There grew in me the dreadful desire to join in the whispering as I had done in the Temple. I bit my lips through and through to still them. All that night the beam shot up through the abyss, the globes swung and the whispering sounded and now I knew the purpose of the caves and of the sculptured figures that still had power to guard them. But what were the people who had carved them? Why had they built their city around the verge and why had they set that Stairway in the pit? What had they been to those Things that dwelt at the bottom and what use had the Things been to them that they should live beside their dwelling place? That there had been some purpose was certain. No work so prodigious as the Stairway would have been undertaken otherwise. But what was the purpose? And why was it that those who had dwelt about the abyss had passed away ages gone, and the dwellers in the abyss still lived? I could find no answer, nor can I find any now. I have not the shred of a theory.

"Dawn came as I wondered and with it silence. I drank what was left of the liquid in my canteen, crept from the cave and began to climb again. That afternoon my legs gave out. I tore off my shirt, made from it pads for my knees and coverings for my hands. I crawled upward. I crawled up and up. And again I crept into one of the caves and waited until again the blue thickened, the shaft of light shot through it and the whispering came.

"But now there was a new note in the whispering. It was no longer threatening. It called and coaxed. It drew.

"A new terror gripped me. There had come upon me a mighty desire to leave the cave and go out where the lights swung; to let them do with me as they pleased, carry me where they wished. The desire grew. It gained fresh impulse with every rise of the beam until at last I vibrated with the desire as I had vibrated to the chant in the Temple. My body was a pendulum. Up would go the beam and I would swing toward it! Only my soul kept steady. It held me fast to the floor of the cave; And all that night it fought with my body against the spell of the pit people.

"Dawn came. Again I crept from the cave and faced the Stairway. I could not rise. My hands were torn and bleeding; my knees an agony. I forced myself upward step by step. After a while my hands became numb, the pain left my knees. They deadened. Step by step my will drove my body upward upon them.

"And then, a nightmare of crawling up infinite stretches of steps, memories of dull horror while hidden within caves with the lights pulsing without and whisperings that called and called me, memory of a time when I awoke to find that my body was obeying the call and had carried me half way out between the guardians of the portals while thousands of gleaming globes rested in the blue haze and watched me."

"Glimpses of bitter fights against sleep and always, always a climb up and up along infinite distances of steps that led from Abaddon to a Paradise of blue sky and open world!

"At last a consciousness of the clear sky close above me, the lip of the pit before me - memory of passing between the great portals of the pit and of steady withdrawal from it - dreams of giant men with strange peaked crowns and veiled faces who pushed me onward and onward and held back Roman Candle globules of light that sought to draw me back to a gulf wherein planets swam between the branches of red trees that had snakes for crowns.

"And then a long, long sleep- how long God alone knows- in a cleft of rocks; an awakening to see far in the North the beam still rising and falling, the lights still hunting, the whispering high above me calling.

"Again crawling on dead arms and legs that moved - that moved like the Ancient Mariner's ship without volition of mine, but that carried me from a haunted place. And then, your fire and this safety!"

The crawling man smiled at us for a moment. Then swiftly life faded from his face. He slept.

That afternoon we struck camp and carrying the crawling man started back South. For three days we carried him and still he slept. And on the third day, still sleeping, he died. We built a great pile of wood and we burned his body as he had asked. We scattered his ashes about the forest with the ashes of the trees that had consumed him. It must be a great magic indeed that could disentangle those ashes and draw him back in a rushing cloud to the pit he called Accursed. I do not think that even the People of the Pit have such a spell. No.

But we did not return to the five peaks to see.

THE END

Three Lines of Old French

"But rich as was the war for surgical science," ended Hawtry, "opening up through mutilation and torture unexplored regions which the genius of man was quick to enter, and, entering, found ways to checkmate suffering and death; for always, my friend, the distillate from the blood of sacrifice is progress, great as all this was, the world tragedy has opened up still another region wherein even greater knowledge will be found. It was the clinic unsurpassed for the psychologist even more than for the surgeon."

Latour, the great little French doctor, drew himself out of the depths of the big chair; the light from the fireplace fell ruddily upon his keen face.

"That is true," he said. "Yes, that is true. There in the furnace the mind of man opened like a flower beneath a too glowing sun. Beaten about in that colossal tempest of primitive forces, caught in the chaos of energies both physical and psychical, which, although man himself was its creator, made of their maker a moth in a whirlwind - all those obscure, those mysterious factors of mind which men, for lack of knowledge, have named the soul, were stripped of their inhibitions and given power to appear.

"How could it have been otherwise; when men and women, gripped by one shattering sorrow or joy, will manifest the hidden depths of spirit; how could it have been otherwise in that steadily maintained crescendo of emotion?" McAndrews spoke.

"Just which psychological region do you mean, Hawtry?" he asked.

There were four of us in front of the fireplace of the Science Club; Hawtry, who rules the chair of psychology in one of our greatest colleges, and whose name is an honored one throughout the world; Latour, an immortal of France; McAndrews, the famous American surgeon whose work during the war has written a new page in the shining book of science; and myself. These are not the names of the three, but they are as I have described them; and I am pledged to identify them no further.

"I mean the field of suggestion," replied the psychologist.

"The mental reactions which reveal themselves as visions, an accidental formation in the clouds that becomes to the over-wrought imaginations of the beholders the so-eagerly-prayed-for hosts of Joan of Arc marching out from heaven; moonlight in the cloud rift that becomes to the besieged a fiery cross held by the hands of archangels; the despair and hope that are transformed into such a legend as the bowmen of Mons, ghostly archers who with their phantom shafts overwhelm the conquering enemy; wisps of cloud over No Man's Land that are translated by the tired eyes of those who peer out into the shape of the Son of Man himself walking sorrowfully among the dead. Signs, portents, and miracles, the hosts of premonitions, of apparitions of loved ones, all dwellers in this land of suggestion; all born of the tearing loose of the veils of the subconscious. Here, when even a thousandth part is gathered, will be work for the psychological analyst for twenty years."

"And the boundaries of this region?" asked McAndrews.

"Boundaries?" Hawtry plainly was perplexed.

McAndrews for a moment was silent. Then he drew from his pocket a yellow slip of paper, a cablegram.

"Young Peter Laveller died today," he said, apparently irrelevantly. "Died where he had set forth to pass, in the remnants of the trenches that cut through the ancient domain of the Seigniors of Tocquelain, up near Bethune."

"Died there!" Hawtry's astonishment was profound. "But I read that he had been brought home; that, indeed, he was one of your triumphs, McAndrews!"

"I said he went there to die," repeated the surgeon slowly.

So that explained the curious reticence of the Lavellers as to what had become of their soldier son, a secrecy which had puzzled the press for weeks. For young Peter Laveller was one of the nation's heroes. The only boy of old Peter Laveller - and neither is that the real name of the family, for, like the others, I may not reveal it - he was the heir to the grim old coal king's millions, and the secret, best loved pulse of his heart.

Early in the war he had enlisted with the French. His father's influence might have abrogated the law of the French army that every man must start from the bottom up - I do not know - but young Peter would have none of it. Steady of purpose, burning with the white fire of the first Crusaders, he took his place in the ranks.

Clean-cut, blue-eyed, standing six feet in his stocking feet, just twenty-five, a bit of a dreamer, perhaps, he was one to strike the imagination of the poilus, and they loved him. Twice was he wounded in the perilous days, and when America came into the war he was transferred to our expeditionary forces. It was at the siege of Mount Kemmel that he received the wounds that brought him back to his father and sister. McAndrews had accompanied him overseas, I knew, and had patched him together - or so all thought.

What had happened then; and why had Laveller gone back to France, to die, as McAndrews put it?

He thrust the cablegram back into his pocket.

"There is a boundary, John," he said to Hawtry. "Laveller's was a borderland case. I'm going to tell it to you." He hesitated. "I ought not to, maybe; and yet I have an idea that Peter would like it told; after all, he believed himself a discoverer." Again he paused; then definitely made up his mind, and turned to me.

"Merritt, you may make use of this if you think it interesting enough. But if you do so decide, then change the names, and be sure to check description short of any possibility of ready identification. After all, it is what happened that is important; and those to whom it happened do not matter."

I promised, and I have observed my pledge. I tell the story as he whom I call McAndrews reconstructed it for us there in the shadowed room, while we sat silent until he had ended.

Laveller stood behind the parapet of a first-line trench. It was night - an early April night in northern France - and when that is said, all is said to those who have been there.

Beside him was a trench periscope. His gun lay touching it. The periscope is practically useless at night; so through a slit in the sand-bags he peered out over the three-hundred-foot-wide stretch of No Man's Land.

Opposite him he knew that other eyes lay close to similar slits in the German parapet, watchful as his were for the least movement.

There were grotesque heaps scattered about No Man's Land, and when the star-shells burst and flooded it with their glare these heaps seemed to stir to move - some to raise themselves, some to gesticulate, to protest. And this was very horrible, for those who moved under the lights were the dead - French and English, Prussian and Bavarian - dregs of a score of carryings to the red wine-press of war set up in this sector.

There were two Jocks on the entanglements; kilted Scots, one colandered by machine-gun hail just as he was breaking through. The shock of the swift, manifold death had hurled his left arm about the neck of the comrade close beside him; and this man had been stricken within the same second. There they leaned, embracing and as the star-shells flared and died, flared and died, they seemed to rock, to try to break from the wire, to dash forward, to return.

Laveller was weary, weary beyond all understanding. The sector was a bad one and nervous. For almost seventy-two hours he had been without sleep for the few minutes now and then of dead stupor broken by constant alarms was worse than sleep.

The shelling had been well-nigh continuous, and the food scarce and perilous to get; three miles back through the fire they had been forced to go for it; no nearer than that could the ration dumps be brought.

And constantly the parapets had to be rebuilt and the wires re-paired and when this was done the shells destroyed again, and once more the dreary routine had to be gone through; for the orders were to hold this sector at all costs.

All that was left of Laveller's consciousness was concentrated in his eyes; only his seeing faculty lived. And sight, obeying the rigid, in-exorable will commanding every reserve of vitality to concentrate on the

34

duty at hand, was blind to everything except the strip before it that Laveller must watch until relieved. His body was numb; he could not feel the
ground with his feet, and sometimes he seemed to be floating in air like
the two Scots upon the wire!

Why couldn't they be still? What right had men whose blood had
drained away into a black stain beneath them to dance and pirouette to
the rhythm of the flares? Damn them, why couldn't a shell drop down
and bury them?

There was a chateau half a mile up there to the right - at least it
had been a chateau. Under it were deep cellars into which one could
creep and sleep. He knew that, because ages ago, when first he had come
into this part of the line, he had slept a night there.

It would be like reentering paradise to crawl again into those cellars, out of the pitiless rain; sleep once more with a roof over his head.

"I will sleep and sleep and sleep - and sleep and sleep and sleep,"
he told himself; then stiffened as at the slumber-compelling repetition of
the word darkness began to gather before him.

The star-shells flared and died, flared and died; the staccato of a
machine gun reached him. He thought that it was his teeth chattering
until his groping consciousness made him realize what it really was -
some nervous German riddling the interminable movement of the dead.

There was a squidging of feet through the chalky mud. No need
to look; they were friends, or they could not have passed the sentries at
the angle of the traverse. Nevertheless, involuntarily, his eyes swept toward the sounds, took note of three cloaked figures regarding him.

There were half a dozen of the lights floating overhead now, and
by the gleams they cast into the trench he recognized the party.

One of them was that famous surgeon who had come over from
the base hospital at Bethune to see made the wounds he healed; the others were his major and his captain; all of them bound for those cellars, no
doubt. Well, some had all the luck! Back went his eyes to the slit.

"What's wrong?" It was the voice of the major addressing the
visitor.

"What's wrong; what's wrong; what's wrong?" The words repeated themselves swiftly, insistently, within his brain, over and over
again, striving to waken it.

Well, what was wrong? Nothing was wrong! Wasn't he, Laveller, there and watching? The tormented brain writhed angrily. Nothing was wrong; why didn't they go away and let him watch in peace?

"Nothing." It was the surgeon…and again the words kept babbling in Laveller's ears, small, whispering, rapidly repeating themselves over and over; "Nothing… nothing… nothing… nothing."

But what was this the surgeon was saying? Fragmentarily, only half understood, the phrases registered:

"Perfect case of what I've been telling you. This lad here, utterly worn, weary, all his consciousness centered upon just one thing - watchfulness . . . consciousness worn to finest point . . . behind it all his subconsciousness crowding to escape . . . consciousness will respond to only one stimulus - movement from without . . . but the subconsciousness, so close to the surface, held so lightly in leash . . . what will it do if that little thread is loosed . . . a perfect case."

What were they talking about? Now they were whispering.

"Then, if I have your permission…" It was the surgeon speaking again. Permission for what? Why didn't they go away and not bother him? Wasn't it hard enough just to watch without having to hear? Some thing passed before his eyes. He looked at it blindly, unrecognizing. His sight must be clouded.

He raised a hand and brushed at his lids. Yes, it must have been his eyes, for it had gone.

A little circle of light glowed against the parapet near his face. It was cast by a small flash. What were they looking for? A hand appeared in the circle, a hand with long, flexible fingers which held a piece of paper on which there was writing. Did they want him to read, too? Not only watch and hear, but read! He gathered himself together to protest.

Before he could force his stiffened lips to move he felt the upper button of his greatcoat undone, a hand slipped through the opening and thrust something into his tunic pocket just above the heart.

Someone whispered "Lucie de Tocquelain." What did it mean? That was not the password. There was a great singing in his head as though he were sinking through water. What was that light that dazzled him even through his closed lids? Painfully he opened his eyes.

Laveller looked straight into the disk of a golden sun slowly setting over a row of noble oaks. Blinded, he dropped his gaze. He was standing ankle-deep in soft, green grass, starred with small clumps of blue flowerets. Bees buzzed about in their chalices. Little yellow-winged butterflies hovered over them. A gentle breeze blew, warm and fragrant.

Oddly he felt no sense of strangeness; then this was a normal home world, a world as it ought to be. But he remembered that he had once been in another world, far, far unlike this; a place of misery and pain, of blood-stained mud and filth, of cold and wet; a world of cruelty, whose nights were tortured hells of glaring lights and fiery, slaying sounds, and tormented men who sought for rest and sleep and found none, and dead who danced. Where was it? Had there ever really been such a world? He was not sleepy now.

He raised his hands and looked at them. They were grimed and cut and stained. He was wearing a greatcoat, wet, mud-bespattered, filthy. High boots were on his legs. Beside one dirt-incrusted foot lay a cluster of the blue flowerets, half-crushed. He groaned in pity, and bent, striving to raise the broken blossoms.

"Too many dead now, too many dead," he whispered; then paused. He had come from that nightmare world! How else in this happy, clean one could he be so unclean?

Of course he had; but where was it? How had he made his way from it here? Ah, there had been a password;what had it been?

He had it: "Lucie de Tocquelain!"

Laveller cried it aloud still kneeling.

A soft little hand touched his cheek. A low, sweet-toned voice caressed his ears.

"I am Lucie de Tocquelain," it said. "And the flowers will grow again yet it is dear of you to sorrow for them."

He sprang to his feet. Beside him stood a girl, a slender maid of eighteen, whose hair was a dusky cloud upon her proud little head and in whose great, brown eyes, resting upon his, tenderness and a half-amused pity dwelt.

Peter stood silent, drinking her in - the low, broad, white forehead; the curved, red lips; the rounded, white shoulders, shining through the silken web of her scarf; the whole lithe sweet body of her in the clinging, quaintly fashioned gown, with its high, clasping girdle.

She was fair enough; but to Peter's starved eyes she was more than that; she was a spring gushing from the arid desert, the first cool breeze of twilight over a heat-drenched isle, the first glimpse of paradise to a soul fresh risen from centuries of hell. And under the burning worship of his eyes her own dropped; a faint rose stained the white throat, crept to her dark hair.

"I... I am the Demoiselle de Tocquelain, messire," she murmured. "And you... "

He recovered his courtesy with a shock. "Laveller... Peter Laveller is my name, mademoiselle," he stammered. "Pardon my rudeness, but how I came here I know not, nor from whence, save that it was... it was a place unlike this. And you... you are so beautiful, mademoiselle!"

The clear eyes raised themselves for a moment, a touch of roguishness in their depths, then dropped demurely once more, but the blush deepened.

He watched her, all his awakening heart in his eyes; then perplexity awoke, touched him insistently.

"Will you tell me what place this is, mademoiselle," he faltered, "and how I came here, if you... " He stopped. From far, far away, from league upon league of space, a vast weariness was sweeping down upon him. He sensed it coming... closer, closer; it touched him; it lapped about him; he was sinking under it; being lost... falling... falling...

Two soft, warm hands gripped his. His tired head dropped upon them. Through the little palms that clasped so tightly pulsed rest and strength. The weariness gathered itself, began to withdraw slowly, so slowly... and was gone!

In its wake followed an ineffable, an uncontrollable desire to weep... to weep in relief that the weariness had passed, that the devil world whose shadows still lingered in his mind was behind him, and that he was here with this maid. And his tears fell, bathing the little hands.

Did he feel her head bent to his, her lips touch his hair? Peace came to him. He rose shamefacedly.

"I do not know why I wept, mademoiselle... " he began; and then saw that her white fingers were clasped now in his blackened ones. He released them in sudden panic.

"I am sorry," he stammered. "I ought not touch you... "

She reached out swiftly, took his hands again in hers, patted them half savagely.

Her eyes flashed.

"I do not see them as you do, Messire Pierre," she answered. "And if I did, are not their stains to me as the stains from hearts of her brave sons on the gonfalons of France? Think no more of your stains save as decorations, messire."

France... France? Why, that was the name of the world he had left behind; the world where men sought vainly for sleep, and the dead danced.

The dead danced... what did that mean? He turned wistful eyes to her.

And with a little cry of pity she clung to him for a moment.

"You are so tired... and you are so hungry," she mourned. "And think no more, nor try to remember, messire, till you have eaten and drunk with us and rested for a space."

They had turned. And now Laveller saw not far away a chateau. It was pinnacled and stately, serene in its gray stone and lordly with its spires and slender turrets thrust skyward from its crest like plumes flung high from some proud prince's helm. Hand in hand like children the Demoiselle de Tocquelain and Peter Laveller approached it over the greensward.

"It is my home, messire," the girl said. "And there among the roses my mother awaits us. My father is away, and he will be sorrowful that he met you not, but you shall meet him when you return."

He was to return, then? That meant he was not to stay. But where was he to go... whence was he to return? His mind groped blindly; cleared again. He was walking among roses; there were roses everywhere, great, fragrant, opened blooms of scarlets and of saffrons, of shell pinks and white; clusters and banks of them, climbing up the terraces, masking the base of the chateau with perfumed tide.

And as he and the maid, still hand in hand, passed between them, they came to a table dressed with snowy napery and pale porcelains beneath a bower.

A woman sat there. She was a little past the prime of life, Peter thought. Her hair, he saw, was powdered white, her cheeks as pink and white as a child's, her eyes the sparkling brown of those of the demoiselle... and gracious... gracious, Peter thought, as some grande dame of old France.

The demoiselle dropped her a low curtsy.

39

"Ma mere," she said, "I bring you the Sieur Pierre la Valliere, a very brave and gallant gentleman who has come to visit us for a little while."

The clear eyes of the older woman scanned him, searched him. Then the stately white head bowed, and over the table a delicate hand was stretched toward him.

It was meant for him to kiss, he knew, but he hesitated awkwardly, miserably, looking at his begrimed own.

"The Sieur Pierre will not see himself as we do," the girl said in half merry reproof; then she laughed, a caressing, golden chiming, "Ma mere, shall he see his hands as we do?"

The white-haired woman smiled and nodded, her eyes kindly and, Laveller noted, with that same pity in them as had been in those of the demoiselle when first he had turned and beheld her.

The girl touched Peter's eyes lightly, held his palms up before him; they were white and fine and clean and in some unfamiliar way beautiful!

Again the indefinable amaze stifled him, but his breeding told. He conquered the sense of strangeness, bowed from the hips, took the dainty fingers of the stately lady in his, and raised them to his lips.

She struck a silver bell. Through the roses came two tall men in livery, who took from Laveller his greatcoat. They were followed by four small black boys in gay scarlet slashed with gold. They bore silver platters on which were meat and fine white bread and cakes, fruit, and wine in tall crystal flagons.

And Laveller remembered how hungry he was. But of that feast he remembered little, up to a certain point. He knows that he sat there filled with a happiness and content that surpassed the sum of happiness of all his twenty-five years.

The mother spoke little, but the Demoiselle Lucie and Peter Laveller chattered and laughed like children, when they were not silent and drinking each the other in.

And ever in Laveller's heart an adoration for this maid, met so perplexingly, grew, grew until it seemed that his heart could not hold his joy. Ever the maid's eyes as they rested on his were softer, more tender, filled with promise; and the proud face beneath the snowy hair became, as it watched them, the essence of that infinitely gentle sweetness that is the soul of the madonnas.

At last the Demoiselle de Tocquelain, glancing up and meeting that gaze, blushed, cast down her long lashes, and hung her head; then raised her eyes bravely.

"Are you content, my mother?" she asked gravely.. "My daughter, I am well content," came the smiling answer.

Swiftly followed the incredible, the terrible, in that scene of beauty and peace it was, said Laveller, like the flashing forth of a gorilla's paw upon a virgin's breast, a wail from deepest hell lancing through the song of angels.

At his right, among the roses, a light began to gleam - a fitful, flaring light that glared and died, glared and died. In it were two shapes. One had an arm clasped about the neck of the other; they leaned embracing in the light, and as it waxed and waned they seemed to pirouette, to try to break from it, to dash forward, to return to dance!

The dead who danced!

A world where men sought rest and sleep, and could find neither, and where even the dead could find no rest, but must dance to the rhythm of the star-shells!

He groaned; sprang to his feet; watched, quivering in every nerve. Girl and woman followed his rigid gaze; turned to him again with tear-filled, pitiful eyes.

"It is nothing!" said the maid. "It is nothing! See, there is nothing there!"

Once more she touched his lids; and the light and the swaying forms were gone. But now Laveller knew. Back into his consciousness rushed the full tide of memory - memory of the mud and the filth, the stenches, and the fiery, slaying sounds, the cruelty, the misery and the hatreds; memory of torn men and tormented dead; memory of whence he had come, the trenches.

The trenches! He had fallen asleep, and all this was but a dream! He was sleeping at his post, while his comrades were trusting him to watch over them. And those two ghastly shapes among the roses; they were the two Scots on the wires summoning him back to his duty; beckoning, beckoning him to return. He must waken! He must waken!

Desperately he strove to drive himself from his garden of illusion; to force himself back to that devil world which during this hour of enchantment had been to his mind only as a fog bank on a far horizon. And as he struggled, the brown-eyed maid and the snowy-tressed woman watched with ineffable pity, tears falling.

"The trenches!" gasped Laveller. "O God, wake me up! I must get back! O God, make me wake."

"Am I only a dream, then, ma mie?"

It was the Demoiselle Lucie's voice a bit piteous, the golden tones shaken.

"I must get back," he groaned, although at her question his heart seemed to die within him. "Let me wake!"

"Am I a dream?" Now the voice was angry; the demoiselle drew close. "Am I not real?"

A little foot stamped furiously on his, a little hand darted out, pinched him viciously close above his elbow. He felt the sting of the pain and rubbed it, gazing at her stupidly.

"Am I a dream, think you?" she murmured, and, raising her palms, set them on his temples, bringing down his head until his eyes looked straight into hers.

Laveller gazed, gazed down, down deep into their depths, lost himself in them, felt his heart rise like the spring from what he saw there. Her warm, sweet breath fanned his cheek; whatever this was, wherever he was, she was no dream!

"But I must return, get back to my trench!" The soldier in him clung to the necessity.

"My son", it was the mother speaking now, "my son, you are in your trench."

Laveller gazed at her, bewildered. His eyes swept the lovely scene about him. When he turned to her again it was with the look of a sorely perplexed child. She smiled.

"Have no fear," she said. "Everything is well. You are in your trench, but your trench centuries ago; yes, twice a hundred years ago, counting time as you do, and as once we did."

A chill ran through him. Were they mad? Was he mad? His arm slipped down over a soft shoulder; the touch steadied him.

"And you?" he forced himself to ask. He caught a swift glance between the two, and in answer to some unspoken question the mother nodded. The Demoiselle Lucie pressed soft hands against Peter's face, looked again into his eyes.

"Ma mie," she said gently, "we have been", she hesitated, "what you call dead to your world these two hundred years!"

But before she had spoken the words Laveller, I think, had sensed what was coming. And if for a fleeting instant he had felt a touch of ice in every vein, it vanished beneath the exaltation that raced through him, vanished as frost beneath a mist-scattering sun. For if this were true, why, then there was no such thing as death! And it was true!

It was true! He knew it with a shining certainty that had upon it not the shadow of a shadow, but how much his desire to believe entered into this certainty who can tell?

He looked at the chateau. Of course! It was that whose ruins loomed out of the darkness when the flares split the night, in whose cellars he had longed to sleep. Death... oh, the foolish, fearful hearts of men!... this death? This glorious place of peace and beauty? And this wondrous girl whose brown eyes were the keys of heart's desire! Death... he laughed and laughed again.

Another thought struck him, swept through him like a torrent. He must get back, must get back to the trenches and tell them this great truth he had found. Why, he was like a traveler from a dying world who unwittingly stumbles upon a secret to turn that world dead to hope into a living heaven!

There was no longer need for men to fear the splintering shell, the fire that seared them, the bullets, or the shining steel. What did they matter when this... this... was the truth? He must get back and tell them. Even those two Scots would lie still on the wires when he --ered this to them.

But he forgot; they knew now. But they could not return to tell, as he could. He was wild with joy, exultant, lifted up to the skies, a demi-god - the bearer of a truth that would free the devil-ridden world from its demons; a new Prometheus who bore back to mankind a more precious flame than had the old.

"I must go!" he cried. "I must tell them! Show me how to return swiftly!"

A doubt assailed him; he pondered it.

"But they may not believe me," he --ered. "No. I must show them proof. I must carry something back to prove this to them."

The Lady of Tocquelain smiled. She lifted a little knife from the table and, reaching over to a rose-tree, cut from it a cluster of buds; thrust it toward his eager hand.

Before he could grasp it the maid had taken it.

"Wait!" she murmured. "I will give you another message."

There was a quill and ink upon the table, and Peter wondered how they had come; he had not seen them before, but with so many wonders, what was this small one? There was a slip of paper in the Demoiselle Lucie's hand, too. She bent her little, dusky head and wrote; blew upon the paper, waved it in the air to dry; sighed, smiled at Peter, and wrapped it about the stem of the rosebud cluster; placed it on the table, and waved back Peter's questing hand.

"Your coat," she said. "You'll need it, for now you must go back."

She thrust his arms into the garment. She was laughing, but there were tears in the great, brown eyes; the red mouth was very wistful.

Now the older woman arose, stretched out her hand again; Laveller bent over it, kissed it.

"We shall be here waiting for you, my son," she said softly. "When it is time for you to come back."

He reached for the roses with the paper wrapped about their stem. The maid darted a hand over his, lifted them before he could touch them.

"You must not read it until you have gone," she said and again the rose flame burned throat and cheeks.

Hand in hand, like children, they sped over the greensward to where Peter had first met her. There they stopped, regarding each other gravely and then that other miracle which had happened to Laveller and that he had forgotten in the shock of his wider realization called for utterance.

"I love you!" whispered Peter Laveller to this living, long-dead Demoiselle de Tocquelain.

She sighed, and was in his arms.

"Oh, I know you do!" she cried. "I know you do, dear one but I was so afraid you would go without telling me so."

She raised her sweet lips, pressed them long to his; drew back.

"I loved you from the moment I saw you standing here," she told him, "and I will be here waiting for you when you return. And now you must go, dear love of mine; but wait "

He felt a hand steal into the pocket of his tunic, press something over his heart.

"The messages," she said. "Take them. And remember I will wait. I promise. I, Lucie de Tocquelain "

There was a singing in his head. He opened his eyes. He was back in his trench, and in his ears still rang the name of the demoiselle, and over his heart he felt still the pressure of her hand. His head was half turned toward three men who were regarding him.

One of them had a watch in his hand; it was the surgeon. Why was he looking at his watch? Had he been gone long? he wondered.

Well, what did it matter, when he was the bearer of such a message? His weariness had gone; he was transformed, jubilant; his soul was shouting paeans. Forgetting discipline, he sprang toward the three.

"There is no such thing as death!" he cried. "We must send this message along the lines at once! At once, do you understand! Tell it to the world I have proof."

He stammered and choked in his eagerness. The three glanced at each other. His major lifted his electric flash, clicked it in Peter's face, started oddly, then quietly walked over and stood between the lad and his rifle.

"Just get your breath a moment, my boy, and then tell us all about it," he said.

They were devilishly unconcerned, were they not? Well, wait till they had heard what he had to tell them!

And tell them Peter did, leaving out only what had passed between him and the demoiselle--for, after all, wasn't that their own personal affair? And gravely and silently they listened to him. But always the trouble deepened in his major's eyes as Laveller poured forth the story.

"And then I came back, came back as quickly as I could, to help us all; to lift us out of all this" his hands swept out in a wide gesture of disgust "for none of it matters! When we die we live!" he ended.

Upon the face of the man of science rested profound satisfaction.

"A perfect demonstration; better than I could ever have hoped!" he spoke over Laveller's head to the major. "Great, how great is the imagination of man!"

There was a tinge of awe in his voice.

Imagination? Peter was cut to the sensitive, vibrant soul of him.

They didn't believe him! He would show them!

"But I have the proof!" he cried.

He threw open his greatcoat, ran his hand into his tunic-pocket; his fingers closed over a bit of paper wrapped around a stem. Ah, now he would show them!

He drew it out, thrust it toward them.

"Look!" His voice was like a triumphal trumpet-call.

What was the matter with them? Could they not see? Why did their eyes search his face instead of realizing what he was offering them? He looked at what he held then, incredulous; brought it close to his own eyes gazed and gazed, with a sound in his ears as though the universe were slipping away around him, with a heart that seemed to have forgotten to beat. For in his hand, stem wrapped in paper, was no fresh and fragrant rosebud cluster his brown-eyed demoiselle's mother had clipped for him in the garden.

No, there was but a sprig of artificial buds, worn and torn and stained, faded and old!

A great numbness crept over Peter.

Dumbly he looked at the surgeon, at his captain, at the major whose face was now troubled indeed and somewhat stern.

"What does it mean?" he muttered.

Had it all been a dream? Was there no radiant Lucie, save in his own mind, no brown-eyed maid who loved him and whom he loved?

The scientist stepped forward, took the worn little sprig from the relaxed grip. The bit of paper slipped off, remained in Peter's fingers.

"You certainly deserve to know just what you've been through, my boy," the urbane, capable voice beat upon his dulled hearing, "after such a reaction as you have provided to our little experiment." He laughed pleasantly.

Experiment? Experiment? A dull rage began to grow in Peter, vicious, slowly rising.

"Messieur!" called the major appealingly, somewhat warningly, it seemed, to his distinguished visitor.

"Oh, by your leave, major," went on the great man, "here is a lad of high intelligence, of education, you could know that by the way he expressed himself, he will understand."

The major was not a scientist, he was a Frenchman, human, and with an imagination of his own. He shrugged; but he moved a little closer to the resting rifle.

"We had been discussing, your officers and I," the capable voice went on, "dreams that are the half-awakened mind's effort to explain some touch, some unfamiliar sound, or what not that has aroused it from its sleep. One is slumbering, say, and a window nearby is broken. The sleeper hears, the consciousness endeavors to learn, but it has given over its control to the subconscious. And this rises accommodatingly to its mate's assistance. But it is irresponsible, and it can express itself only in pictures.

"It takes the sound and... well, weaves a little romance around it. It does its best to explain... alas! Its best is only a more or less fantastic lie recognized as such by the consciousness the moment it becomes awake.

"And the movement of the subconsciousness in this picture production is inconceivably rapid. It can depict in the fraction of a second a series of incidents that if actually lived would take hours... yes, days of time. You follow me, do you not? Perhaps you recognize the experience I outline?"

Laveller nodded. The bitter, consuming rage was mounting within him steadily. But he was outwardly calm, all alert. He would hear what this self-satisfied devil had done to him, and then...

"Your officers disagreed with some of my conclusions. I saw you here, weary, concentrated upon the duty at hand, half in hypnosis from the strain and the steady flaring and dying of the lights. You offered a perfect clinical subject, a laboratory test unexcelled."

Could he keep his hands from his throat until he had finished? Laveller wondered. Lucie, his Lucie, a fantastic lie.

"Steady, mon vieux", it was his major whispering. Ah, when he struck, he must do it quickly, his officer was too close, too close. Still, he must keep his watch for him through the slit. He would be peering there, perhaps, when he, Peter, leaped.

"And so", the surgeon's tones were in his best student-clinic manner, "and so I took a little sprig of artificial flowers that I had found pressed between the leaves of an old missal I had picked up in the ruins of the chateau yonder. On a slip of paper I wrote a line of French; for then I thought you a French soldier. It was a simple line from the ballad of Aucassin and Nicolette. "

And there she waits to greet him when all his days are run.

"Also, there was a name written on the title-page of the missal, the name, no doubt, of its long-dead owner - 'Lucie de Tocquelain'"

Lucie! Peter's rage and hatred were beaten back by a great surge of longing rushed back stronger than ever.

"So I passed the sprig of flowers before your unseeing eyes; consciously unseeing, I mean, for it was certain your subconsciousness would take note of them. I showed you the line of writing, your subconsciousness absorbed this, too, with its suggestion of a love troth, a separation, an awaiting. I wrapped it about the stem of the sprig, I thrust them both into your pocket, and called the name of Lucie de Tocquelain into your ear.

"The problem was what your other self would make of those four things, the ancient cluster, the suggestion in the line of writing, the touch, and the name - a fascinating problem, indeed!

"And hardly had I withdrawn my hand, almost before my lips closed on the word I had whispered, you had turned to us shouting that there was no such thing as death, and pouring out, like one inspired, that remarkable story of yours - all, all built by your imagination from."

But he got no further. The searing rage in Laveller had burst all bounds, had flared forth murderously and hurled him silently at the surgeon's throat. There were flashes of flame before his eyes; red, sparkling sheets of flame. He would die for it, but he would kill this cold-blooded fiend who could take a man out of hell, open up to him heaven, and then thrust him back into hell grown now a hundred times more cruel, with all hope dead in him for eternity.

Before he could strike strong hands gripped him, held him fast. The scarlet, curtained flares before his eyes faded away. He thought he heard a tender, golden voice whispering to him:

"It is nothing! It is nothing! See as I do!"

He was standing between his officers, who held him fast on each side. They were silent, looking at the now white-faced surgeon with more than somewhat of cold, unfriendly sternness in their eyes.

"My boy, my boy", that scientist's poise was gone; his voice trembling, agitated. "I did not understand... I am sorry... I never thought you would take it so seriously."

Laveller spoke to his officers----ly. "It is over, sirs. You need not hold me."

They looked at him, released him, patted him on the shoulder, fixed again their visitor with that same utter contempt.

Laveller turned stumblingly to the parapet. His eyes were full of tears. Brain and heart and soul were nothing but a blind desolation, a waste utterly barren of hope or of even the ghost of the wish to hope. That message of his, the sacred truth that was to set the feet of a tormented world on the path to paradise, a dream.

His Lucie, his brown-eyed demoiselle who had murmured her love for him, a thing compounded of a word, a touch, a writing, and an artificial flower!

He could not, would not believe it. Why, he could feel still the touch of her soft lips on his, her warm body quivering in his arms. And she had said he would come back, and promised to wait for him.

What was that in his hand? It was the paper that had wrapped the rosebuds, the cursed paper with which that cold devil had experimented with him.

Laveller crumpled it savagely, raised it to hurl it at his feet.

Someone seemed to stay his hand.

Slowly he opened it.

The three men watching him saw a glory steal over his face, a radiance like that of a soul redeemed from endless torture. All its sorrow, its agony, was wiped out, leaving it a boy's once more.

He stood wide-eyed, dreaming.

The major stepped forward, gently drew the paper from Laveller.

There were many star-shells floating on high now, the trench was filled with their glare, and in their light he scanned the fragment.

On his face when he raised it there was a great awe, and as they took it from him and read this same awe dropped down upon the others like a veil.

For over the line the surgeon had written were now three other lines in old French.

Nor grieve, dear heart, nor fear the seeming. Here is waking after dreaming.

She who loves you, Lucie.

That was McAndrews's story, and it was Hawtry who finally broke the silence that followed his telling of it.

"The lines had been on the paper, of course," he said; "they were probably faint, and your surgeon had not noticed them. It was drizzling, and the dampness brought them out."

"No," answered McAndrews; "they had not been there."

"But how can you be so sure?" remonstrated the Psychologist.

"Because I was the surgeon," said McAndrews quietly. "The paper was a page torn from my note book. When I wrapped it about the sprig it was blank, except for the line I myself had written there.

"But there was one more bit of... well, shall we call it evidence, John?... the hand in which Laveller's message was penned was the hand in the missal in which I had found the flowers and the signature 'Lucie' was that same signature, curve for curve and quaint, old-fashioned angle for angle."

A longer silence fell, broken once more by Hawtry, abruptly.

"What became of the paper?" he asked. "Was the ink analyzed? Was..."

"As we stood there wondering," interrupted McAndrews, "a squall swept down upon the trench. It tore the paper from my hand; carried it away. Laveller watched it go; made no effort to get it.

"'It does not matter. I know now,' he said and smiled at me, the forgiving, happy smile of a joyous boy. 'I apologize to you, doctor. You're the best friend I ever had. I thought at first you had done to me what no other man would do to another I see now that you have done for me what no other man could.'

50

"And that is all. He went through the war neither seeking death nor avoiding it. I loved him like a son. He would have died after that Mount Kemmel affair had it not been for me. He wanted to live long enough to bid his father and sister goodby, and I patched him up. He did it, and then set forth for the trench beneath the shadow of the ruined old chateau where his brown-eyed demoiselle had found him."

"Why?" asked Hawtry.

"Because he thought that from there he could go back to her more quickly."

"To me an absolutely unwarranted conclusion," said the psychologist, wholly irritated, half angry. "There is some simple, natural explanation of it all."

"Of course, John," answered McAndrews soothingly "of course there is. Tell us it, can't you?"

But Hawtry, it seemed, could not offer any particulars.

THE END

Also from Benediction Books …

Wandering Between Two Worlds: Essays on Faith and Art
Anita Mathias

Benediction Books, 2007
152 pages
ISBN: 0955373700

Available from www.amazon.com, www.amazon.co.uk

In these wide-ranging lyrical essays, Anita Mathias writes, in lush, lovely prose, of her naughty Catholic childhood in Jamshedpur, India; her large, eccentric family in Mangalore, a sea-coast town converted by the Portuguese in the sixteenth century; her rebellion and atheism as a teenager in her Himalayan boarding school, run by German missionary nuns, St. Mary's Convent, Nainital; and her abrupt religious conversion after which she entered Mother Teresa's convent in Calcutta as a novice. Later rich, elegant essays explore the dualities of her life as a writer, mother, and Christian in the United States-- Domesticity and Art, Writing and Prayer, and the experience of being "an alien and stranger" as an immigrant in America, sensing the need for roots.

About the Author

Anita Mathias is the author of *Wandering Between Two Worlds: Essays on Faith and Art.* She has a B.A. and M.A. in English from Somerville College, Oxford University, and an M.A. in Creative Writing from the Ohio State University, USA. Anita won a National Endowment of the Arts fellowship in Creative Nonfiction in 1997. She lives in Oxford, England with her husband, Roy, and her daughters, Zoe and Irene.

Anita's website:
   http://www.anitamathias.com, and
Anita's blog Dreaming Beneath the Spires:
   http://dreamingbeneaththespires.blogspot.com

The Church That Had Too Much
Anita Mathias
Benediction Books, 2010
52 pages
ISBN: 9781849026567

Available from www.amazon.com, www.amazon.co.uk

The Church That Had Too Much was very well-intentioned. She wanted to love God, she wanted to love people, but she was both hampered by her muchness and the abundance of her possessions, and beset by ambition, power struggles and snobbery. Read about the surprising way The Church That Had Too Much began to resolve her problems in this deceptively simple and enchanting fable.

About the Author

Anita Mathias is the author of *Wandering Between Two Worlds: Essays on Faith and Art*. She has a B.A. and M.A. in English from Somerville College, Oxford University, and an M.A. in Creative Writing from the Ohio State University, USA. Anita won a National Endowment of the Arts fellowship in Creative Nonfiction in 1997. She lives in Oxford, England with her husband, Roy, and her daughters, Zoe and Irene.

Anita's website:
    http://www.anitamathias.com, and
Anita's blog Dreaming Beneath the Spires:
    http://dreamingbeneaththespires.blogspot.com

www.ingramcontent.com/pod-product-compliance
Lightning Source LLC
Chambersburg PA
CBHW050912120626
46552CB00004B/1531